MISSIONS TO MARS

by Gregory L. Vogt

FOCUS READERS

www.focusreaders.com

Focus Readers is distributed by North Star Editions:
sales@northstareditions.com | 888-417-0195

Produced for Focus Readers by Red Line Editorial.

Content Consultant: James Flaten, Associate Director of NASA's MN Space Grant Consortium and Contract Associate Professor, Aerospace Engineering and Mechanics Department, University of Minnesota–Twin Cities

Photographs ©: JPL-Caltech/MSSS/JPL/NASA, cover, 1; Malin Space Science Systems/ JPL/NASA, 4–5; GRC/NASA, 7; JPL-Caltech/JPL/NASA, 9, 30–31, 35; MSFC/NASA, 10–11; JPL-Caltech/University of Arizona/JPL/NASA, 13; KSC/NASA, 14–15, 42–43; NASA, 17; JPL-Caltech/GSFC/University of Arizona/JPL/NASA, 19; Corbis Historical/Getty Images, 21; NASA Jet Propulsion Lab/JPL/AP Images, 22–23; JPL/NASA, 24, 29; JPL-Caltech/University of Arizona/Texas A&M University/JPL/NASA, 27; JPL/Cornell/NASA, 33; Michael Probst/AP Images, 36–37; JPL-Caltech/University of Arizona/University of Leicester/JPL/NASA, 38; Kim Shiflett/KSC/NASA, 41; Refugio Ruiz/AP Images, 45

ISBN
978-1-63517-496-0 (hardcover)
978-1-63517-568-4 (paperback)
978-1-63517-712-1 (ebook pdf)
978-1-63517-640-7 (hosted ebook)

Library of Congress Control Number: 2017948053

Printed in the United States of America
Mankato, MN
November, 2017

ABOUT THE AUTHOR

Gregory L. Vogt is an assistant professor at Baylor College of Medicine in Texas. He has also been a science museum director and an educational specialist in the NASA Astronaut Office.

TABLE OF CONTENTS

CHAPTER 1

REACHING THE RED PLANET

Mars is the fourth planet from the sun. In the night sky, it looks like a reddish star. Known as the Red Planet, it has fascinated astronomers for ages. People often wondered if there was life on Mars. But even the largest telescopes showed only fuzzy views of the planet's surface. To learn more about Mars, people would need to send a spacecraft. But Mars is millions of miles from Earth. Sending a rocket there would be difficult.

Mars is more than 140 million miles (225 million km) from the sun.

The first attempt to send a spacecraft to Mars took place in 1960. The Soviet Union tried to launch a **probe**. But the spacecraft's rockets failed to produce enough power, so the probe fell back to Earth. In 1962, the Soviet Union tried again but still faced problems. Two spacecraft fell apart before leaving Earth's orbit. A third spacecraft successfully headed toward Mars, but scientists lost contact with it before it reached the planet.

The United States soon followed with its own Mars missions. The country's space agency, the National Aeronautics and Space Administration (NASA), launched *Mariner 3* in 1964. But the spacecraft's protective shell would not open. Without this shield, *Mariner 3* could not make the journey to Mars. NASA tried again with *Mariner 4*. This spacecraft traveled through space for eight months. It flew past Mars in July 1965. *Mariner 4*

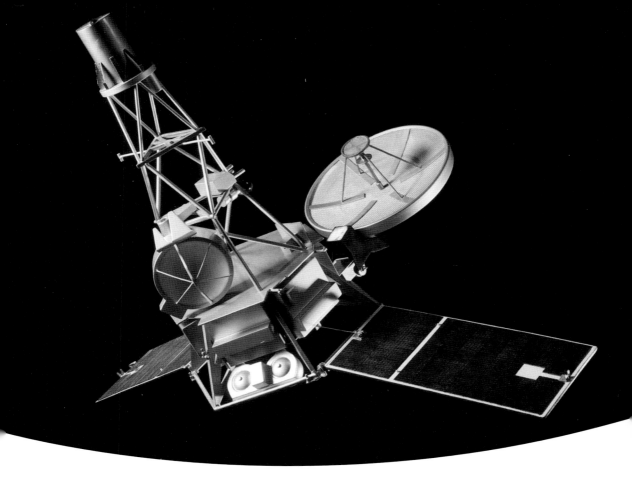

▲ This model shows what *Mariner 4* looked like.

made scientific measurements and took 21 pictures. The fuzzy pictures showed an ancient surface with many **craters**. In 1969, NASA sent two more probes to Mars. *Mariner 6* and *Mariner 7* flew by the planet and took hundreds of pictures.

On November 14, 1971, *Mariner 9* became the first spacecraft to orbit Mars. This probe took more than 7,000 pictures. The images revealed many things about the planet's surface. They showed giant volcanoes many times larger than Earth's biggest mountains. Other photos showed plains, craters, ice caps, and water-cut channels. They even revealed a huge canyon.

Scientists used the photos to make maps of the Martian surface. These maps were important for NASA's next Mars mission. In this mission, NASA hoped to land spacecraft on the planet's surface. The maps helped planners to choose the best landing spots.

Throughout the 1960s, the Soviet Union had also attempted several more missions to Mars. Most of the missions had ended in failure. Finally, two missions in 1971 were partly successful. Each

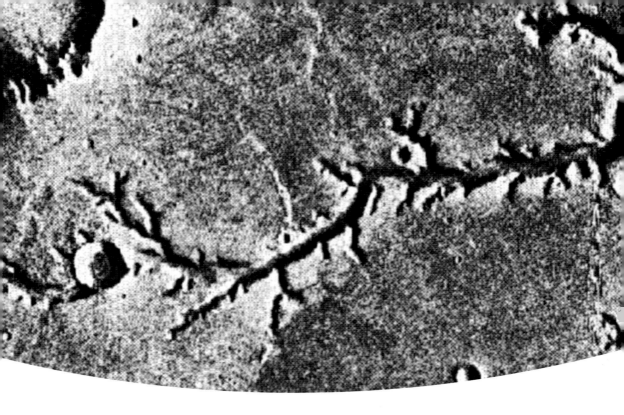

▲ *Mariner 9* photographed channels on the surface of Mars.

mission included a lander that descended to the planet's surface and an **orbiter** that stayed above. *Mars 2* reached Mars on November 27, but its lander crashed on the surface. In December, the *Mars 3* lander descended to the surface. It sent only 20 seconds of data before contact was lost. But it had made the first successful Mars landing.

CHAPTER 2

ORBITERS AND LANDERS

In 1975, NASA launched two spacecraft called *Viking 1* and *Viking 2*. The spacecraft reached Mars nearly one year later. Each spacecraft consisted of an orbiter and a lander. The orbiters stayed in orbit around the planet and took pictures. Meanwhile, the landers entered the **atmosphere**. Parachutes slowed their fall as they descended toward the planet's surface. Just before landing, the parachutes dropped away.

Viking 1 was launched with a Titan III-Centaur rocket on August 20, 1975.

Small rocket engines fired to make the landers slow down and land gently on the planet's surface.

Each lander had three legs. The landers did not have wheels, so they could not move. Instead, each lander used cameras and weather instruments to study the area where it landed. A robotic arm collected samples. It could reach approximately 10 feet (3.0 m) from the lander.

Each lander's arm scooped up Martian soil. The arm dropped small amounts of soil into the lander's science laboratories. These small laboratories were built into the lander. They analyzed the soil. Scientists back on Earth hoped to find signs of microscopic life on Mars.

Viking 1 and *Viking 2* did not find any signs of life. But they helped scientists learn much more about the planet. Both orbiters had cameras that were newer and better than *Mariner 9*'s cameras.

▲ Each Viking lander had two cameras, which were held in cylinder-shaped housings on either side of its antenna.

As a result, the pictures were clearer and showed many more details about the Martian surface. They revealed that the surface was covered with rust-colored dust. The plains were dotted with rocks. Many of these rocks had holes in them, which meant the rocks were probably formed by volcanoes.

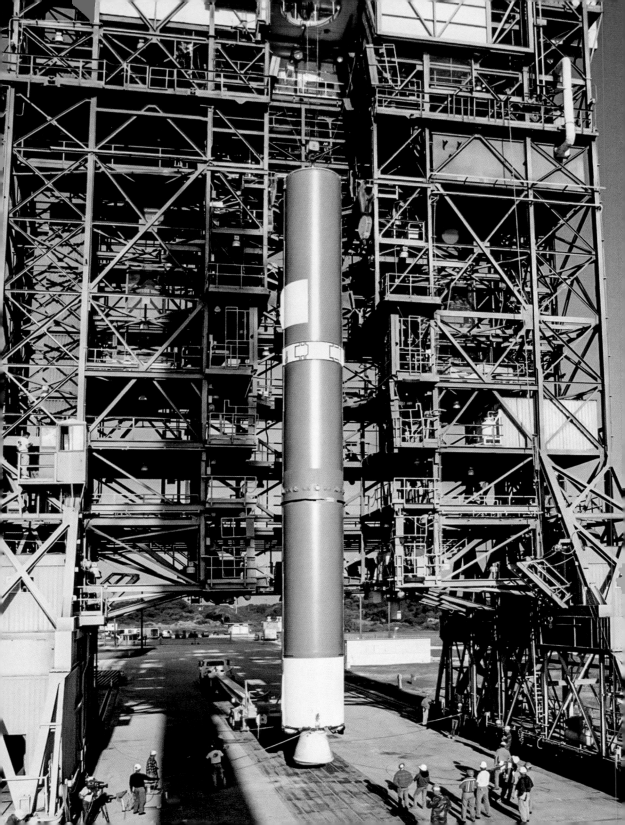

CHAPTER 3

TRIAL AND ERROR

Scientists wanted to return to Mars and explore its surface more thoroughly. But sending a spacecraft to Mars is very challenging. A mission to Mars begins with a rocket launch. However, rockets sometimes explode, and engines sometimes fail. Even after launch, many things can go wrong. Temperatures in space range from extremely cold to very hot. And radiation in space can damage sensitive instruments.

NASA tried using Delta II rockets to launch spacecraft to Mars in the 1990s.

Another challenge is that Earth and Mars are constantly moving. A spacecraft must be aimed at the spot where Mars will be when the spacecraft arrives several months later. It is easy to make navigation errors and miss the planet.

Deciding when to launch the spacecraft is also complicated. When both planets are on the same side of the sun, Mars is approximately 35 million miles (56 million km) away from Earth. When the planets are on opposite sides of the sun, Mars is 250 million miles (402 million km) from Earth.

However, the two planets travel around the sun at different speeds. Mars orbits more slowly. If scientists launched a spacecraft when Earth and Mars were closest together, the spacecraft would have to loop all the way around the sun to reach Mars. This long trip would take two years.

HOW TO GET TO MARS ◄

To reach Mars, a rocket must launch when Earth and Mars are at the correct places in their orbits.

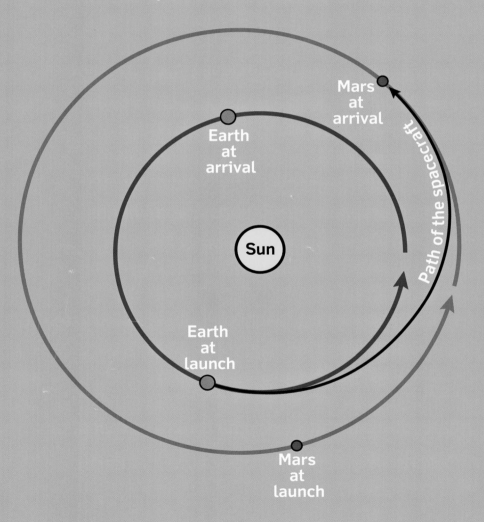

Scientists prefer not to launch a spacecraft when Earth and Mars are closest together. Instead, they try to launch the spacecraft when Mars is ahead of Earth. In this case, the fast-moving spacecraft will catch up to the planet. A spacecraft launched at this time can arrive at Mars after only six or seven months. However, this ideal launch time only occurs every 26 months.

In 1988, the Soviet Union launched two spacecraft known as *Phobos 1* and *Phobos 2*. Scientists hoped to use them to study Phobos, one of Mars's two tiny moons. Unfortunately, neither spacecraft reached Phobos. Scientists on Earth sent a software program to *Phobos 1* as it was on its way to Mars. But the program had a flaw. It shut down the thrusters that kept *Phobos 1*'s antenna properly aimed at Earth. Radio contact with *Phobos 1* was lost as a

▲ Mars (left) has two tiny moons called Phobos (center) and Deimos (right).

result. *Phobos 2* almost reached Phobos. But the spacecraft's computer malfunctioned, and scientists lost contact with it.

The United States launched the Mars Observer spacecraft in 1992. It was designed to orbit Mars and study the planet's **geology** and climate.

The mission started well. However, NASA lost contact with the spacecraft three days before it was supposed to go into orbit. No one is sure what happened. Some engineers think a fuel line for the spacecraft's engines might have burst. Gas escaping from the fuel line would have worked like a rocket thruster. It would have made the spacecraft spin too rapidly to work properly.

Russia attempted to send a mission to Mars in 1996. It consisted of an orbiter, two small landers, and two penetrators. Penetrators are probes that slam into a planet's surface. How deep they go can tell geologists what lies beneath the planet's surface. Unfortunately, these spacecraft never made it to Mars. A problem as the rocket launched caused the spacecraft to fall back to Earth.

Despite numerous challenges, engineers in both Russia and the United States persevered.

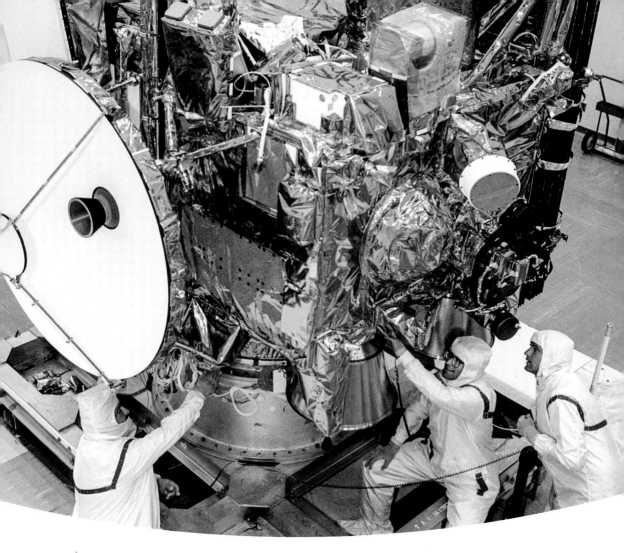

The Mars Observer spacecraft launched on September 25, 1992.

And in 1997, the hard work of NASA engineers paid off with the success of the Mars Pathfinder mission.

CHAPTER 4

STUDYING THE SURFACE

Launched in 1996, the Mars Pathfinder mission brought the first **rover** to Mars. This rover, known as *Sojourner*, was carried inside a lander called *Pathfinder* during the journey to Mars. The lander touched down on the planet's surface in July 1997 and began collecting information about the landing site. Meanwhile, *Sojourner* rolled around the Martian surface. It was the first rover to be used on any planet other than Earth.

Several photos were stitched together to create this image of *Sojourner* on Mars.

▲ *Sojourner* rolled across the surface of Mars for 83 days.

Sojourner weighed 24 pounds (11 kg). It was about the size of a microwave oven. Solar panels covered its flat upper surface. These panels made electricity from sunlight to power the rover. *Sojourner* also carried two cameras and an instrument for determining the chemistry of rocks. An antenna stuck up from the rover as well. *Sojourner* used this antenna to communicate with the lander.

During their mission, *Sojourner* and *Pathfinder* took more than 17,000 pictures. They performed 15 chemical studies of rocks and soil. They also collected extensive data about Martian weather. The two spacecraft made several important discoveries. For instance, they found rounded rocks and rocks made from rounded pebbles. On Earth, rocks with these shapes are formed by running water. For this reason, scientists concluded that Mars might have had running water on its surface at one time.

Scientists wanted to learn more about the climate on Mars. So, in December 1998, NASA launched the Mars Climate Orbiter mission. The Mars Polar Lander mission began one month later.

The spacecraft from these missions were intended to work together when they arrived at Mars. Unfortunately, NASA lost contact with both spacecraft. But scientists continued trying to learn more about the history of water on Mars. In 2002, the Mars Odyssey mission detected traces of frozen water beneath the planet's surface. And in 2008, a lander called *Phoenix* confirmed that underground ice existed.

Phoenix landed near the north pole of Mars. The lander's robotic arm dug through the soil and found water frozen beneath the planet's surface. Then the lander studied the soil and ice for signs

> THINK ABOUT IT

Why would it be important to find evidence of running water on Mars, even if the water existed in the distant past?

▲ *Phoenix*'s mission lasted for three months.

of life. *Phoenix* detected a mineral that suggested the ice might have thawed in the past. It also found other minerals that could have possibly provided nutrients needed for life.

LANDING ON MARS

During the long flight to Mars, the *Sojourner* rover was packed tightly inside the *Pathfinder* lander. When the lander entered the planet's atmosphere, it was enclosed in a two-piece protective shell. The shell shielded the spacecraft from the heat caused by **friction** with the atmosphere. As *Pathfinder* neared the planet's surface, the bottom half of the shell dropped off, and a parachute opened to slow the lander's fall.

Near the ground, *Pathfinder* was lowered on a tether from the upper half of the shell. As the lander lowered, airbags inflated around it like a bunch of balloons. Small rockets briefly stopped the descent, and the tether was cut. Surrounded by airbags, the lander fell the rest of the way to the surface. It bounced 15 times on its airbags. Then it stopped, and the airbags deflated. Next, the lander unfolded. Its instruments were ready

▲ *Sojourner* rolled past the *Pathfinder* lander's deflating airbags to reach the surface of Mars.

to take pictures and collect information about the landing site.

When *Pathfinder* unfolded, *Sojourner* was free to roll across the Martian surface. Its six wheels were driven by electric motors. This six-wheel design enabled the rover to move in any direction. During its mission, *Sojourner* stayed within 40 feet (12 m) of the lander. But the rover rolled a total distance of nearly 330 feet (100 m).

CHAPTER 5

LOOKING FOR WATER AND LIFE

Meanwhile, NASA was developing other rovers. Identical rovers called *Spirit* and *Opportunity* landed on Mars in 2004. Each rover had six wheels and was the size of a golf cart. A tall mast held cameras and scientific instruments. Solar panels fanned to the sides of the mast. A robotic arm with tools and instruments projected from the front. And several antennas let the rover communicate with orbiting spacecraft and Earth.

Models show the sizes of *Spirit* (left), *Sojourner* (middle), and the 2012 rover *Curiosity* (right).

Scientists used the rovers to study rocks and soil. Each rover's cameras showed many details about the planet's rocks. These details could reveal how the rocks formed. For instance, rocks with bubble holes were likely formed by volcanic eruptions. Rocks made up of layers indicate hardened **sediment** from the bottoms of ancient lakes and oceans.

One instrument on the rover's arm was a combination of a microscope and a camera. It provided even closer views of rocks and soil. Another tool on the rover's arm could scrape and drill into rocks. This allowed scientists to see how hard the rocks were and study their interiors.

Spirit and *Opportunity* found more evidence that water once flowed on the planet's surface. For instance, *Opportunity* discovered a mineral vein in 2011. This vein was likely formed by liquid

△ *Spirit* took this photo of the Martian surface.

water. This discovery excited scientists. Liquid water meant microscopic life might have existed on Mars.

The rovers were expected to last only a few months. However, both lasted much longer. In 2009, *Spirit*'s wheels got stuck in soft soil. It could no longer move, but it continued sending information to Earth until 2010. *Opportunity* kept exploring Mars. A new rover, *Curiosity,* joined it in 2012. *Curiosity* was the size of a small car.

Earlier rovers used solar panels to generate power. However, the panels often became covered with dust. That caused them to produce less power. *Curiosity* used a nuclear generator instead. The generator got its power from **radioactive** elements.

Scientists planned for *Curiosity* to operate on Mars for two years. But as of 2017, *Curiosity* was still collecting data about Mars. One tool measures the temperature and wind speed on the planet. It also tracks the humidity and atmospheric pressure. This information helps scientists understand the weather on Mars.

Another instrument sends beams of **neutrons** down through the planet's surface. The way these particles bounce back can indicate if water or ice is underground. *Curiosity* also carries a tool for drilling into rocks. Scientists use this tool to study the material beneath the surface. Samples from the drill holes revealed elements such as carbon, hydrogen, and oxygen. These elements are key ingredients for life.

HOW *CURIOSITY* STUDIES MARS ◄

Mastcam: Takes color images and video of the surface

ChemCam: Uses a laser to study rocks and soil at a distance

RAD: Collects information about radiation on the surface

REMS: Collects information about the atmosphere, wind, and temperature

DAN: Uses neutrons to search for ice beneath the surface

APXS: Measures chemicals in rocks and soil

MARDI: Takes high-resolution video

CHAPTER 6

INTERNATIONAL EXPLORATION

The United States and Russia are not the only nations that have tried sending spacecraft to Mars. In 1998, Japan launched a spacecraft known as *Nozomi*. But control problems prevented the spacecraft from orbiting Mars, so it went into orbit around the sun instead.

The European Space Agency (ESA) has sent a spacecraft to Mars. ESA consists of more than 20 nations that work together to explore space.

Scientists at the European Space Agency monitor their Mars probe in 2003.

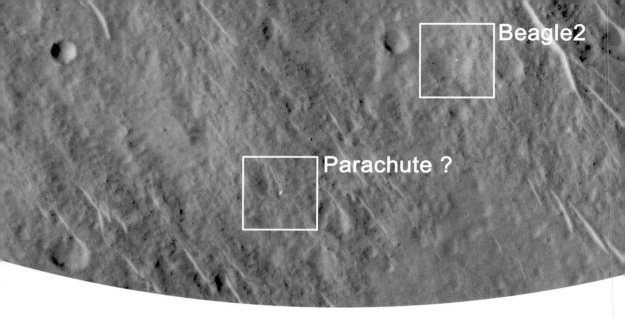

▲ A picture taken by a NASA spacecraft in 2014 showed that *Beagle 2* had landed on Mars.

In 2003, ESA's Mars Express mission sent an orbiter and lander to Mars. The orbiter took detailed pictures of the planet's geology. The *Beagle 2* lander was supposed to study the Martian surface, but ESA lost contact with it.

Twelve years later, *Beagle 2* was spotted on the surface of Mars. It appeared to have landed safely, but it could not communicate with Earth. ESA also launched the ExoMars 2016 mission.

This mission's lander crashed, but its orbiter was a success.

China also attempted to send an orbiter to Mars. Known as *Yinghuo-1*, it launched in 2011. Chinese scientists hoped the orbiter would study the way the Martian atmosphere interacts with outer space. But the orbiter's rocket failed, and it fell back to Earth two months after launch.

India's *Mangalyaan* spacecraft was more successful. It arrived in Martian orbit in 2013. It studied the atmosphere and took many pictures of the planet's surface. Other countries are planning additional missions to Mars.

THINK ABOUT IT ◁

Why do you think there have been more successful orbiter missions than lander missions?

ELLEN STOFAN

Ellen Stofan has space exploration in her blood. She was born in Oberlin, Ohio, in 1961. Her father was Andrew Stofan, a rocket engineer who worked for NASA for many years.

Stofan earned three college degrees. She studied geological sciences. That led her to a job with NASA in the field of planetary exploration. From 1991 to 2000, Stofan worked at NASA's Jet Propulsion Laboratory. She was the chief scientist for the Magellan mission to Venus. Stofan also helped with the Cassini mission to Saturn.

Stofan has a special interest in the possibility of finding life on other planets. In the search for life, Mars is an obvious place to go. Stofan points out that Mars is close to Earth. Scientists know that water has flowed on its surface. Many scientists believe water is essential to life. And some scientists even think that tiny life-forms

⚠ Ellen Stofan has worked on missions to Mars, Saturn, and Venus.

may still exist beneath the Martian soil. Therefore, Stofan believes it is important that humans do not contaminate Mars. Still, she is in favor of sending humans to the planet.

NASA promoted Stofan to chief scientist in 2013. For three years, she advised NASA on science programs and its future directions. Stofan resigned from NASA in 2016. Afterward, she became a speaker on science, space exploration, and social issues.

CHAPTER 7

HUMAN LANDINGS

As of 2017, scientists had not found evidence of current or past life on Mars. But they had learned a lot about the planet. This information has helped them prepare to send humans to Mars. Someday, humans may even create a colony on the planet. Traveling the long distance to Mars would require large rockets and spaceships. So, NASA began working to make powerful rockets. A company called SpaceX designed rockets, too.

NASA conducts tests of Delta IV Heavy rockets, which may eventually carry a spacecraft to Mars.

SpaceX set a goal to land humans on Mars in the 2020s. Eventually, the company planned to establish a permanent colony.

Living on Mars would be difficult for humans. The planet's thin atmosphere is mostly made up of carbon dioxide. However, humans need oxygen for breathing. They would need more oxygen than their spacecraft could carry. One way to solve this problem would be producing oxygen from the planet's resources. For example, NASA made plans for an instrument called MOXIE. This instrument would change carbon dioxide from the Martian atmosphere into breathable air.

> ## ➤ THINK ABOUT IT

How would sending humans to Mars help scientists learn more about the planet?

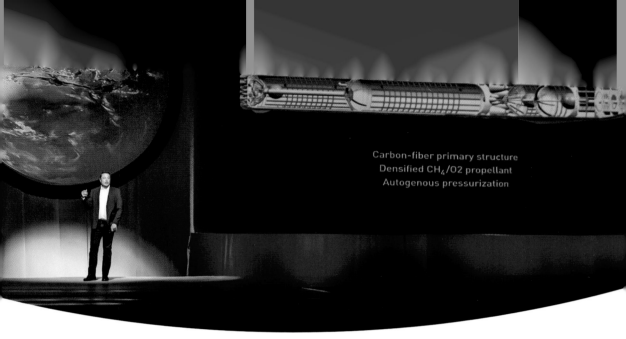

Carbon-fiber primary structure
Densified CH_4/O_2 propellant
Autogenous pressurization

SpaceX planned to develop a rocket that could hold 100 or more people.

In addition, people living on Mars would need a way to clean and recycle water. They might need to grow their own food as well. Some scientists proposed sending robotic spacecraft to Mars. These spacecraft would carry supplies and scientific gear to the planet before the first humans arrived. Then, after years of studying Mars with rovers, humans would finally set foot on the Red Planet.

MISSIONS TO MARS

Write your answers on a separate piece of paper.

1. Write a paragraph explaining why so many missions to Mars have failed.

2. If given the opportunity, would you want to live on Mars? Why or why not?

3. When did the first rover land on Mars?

    A. 1971
    B. 1988
    C. 1997

4. How did sending a lander rather than an orbiter help scientists explore Mars?

    A. A lander could send information back to the scientists on Earth.
    B. A lander could descend to the planet's surface and take detailed pictures.
    C. A lander could carry more scientific instruments because of its larger size.

Answer key on page 48.

GLOSSARY

atmosphere
The layers of gases that surround a planet or moon.

craters
Round or nearly-round holes in the surface of a planet or moon, often caused by asteroid or comet crashes.

friction
A force generated by the rubbing of one thing against another.

geology
The study of a planet or moon's physical structure, especially its layers of soil and rocks.

neutrons
Tiny particles that have no electrical charge and make up part of the nucleus of all atoms but hydrogen.

orbiter
A spacecraft that orbits a planet or moon but does not land on its surface.

probe
A device used to explore.

radioactive
Giving off energy in the form of rays or particles that come from atoms that are breaking apart.

rover
A wheeled spacecraft that rolls across the surface of a planet or moon.

sediment
Stones, sand, or other materials that are carried by flowing water.

TO LEARN MORE

BOOKS

Aldrin, Buzz, and Marianne J. Dyson. *Welcome to Mars: Making a Home on the Red Planet*. Washington, DC: National Geographic, 2015.

Doeden, Matt. *Human Travel to the Moon and Mars: Waste of Money or Next Frontier?* Minneapolis: Twenty-First Century Books, 2012.

Rusch, Elizabeth. *The Mighty Mars Rovers: The Incredible Adventures of Spirit and Opportunity*. Boston: Houghton Mifflin Books for Children, 2012.

NOTE TO EDUCATORS

Visit **www.focusreaders.com** to find lesson plans, activities, links, and other resources related to this title.

INDEX

Answer Key: 1. Answers will vary; **2.** Answers will vary; **3.** C; **4.** B